S Jameson

For Asia, aka Joanna
my inspiration
~EL

Til Daniel og
Hannah fra Tante Jane
~JM

This edition produced for The Book People Ltd
Hall Wood Avenue, Haydock, St Helens WA11 9UL, by
LITTLE TIGER PRESS
1 The Coda Centre, 189 Munster Road, London SW6 6AW

First published in Great Britain 2003

Printed in Singapore • ISBN 1 85430 852 1
1 3 5 7 9 10 8 6 4 2

It's Mine!

Ewa Lipniacka   Jane Massey

TED SMART

“It’s mine!” yelled Jack.
“Mine!” screamed Georgie.

"It belongs to nobody now you've broken it," scolded Mum. "You two must learn to share!"

In the garden Georgie shared
her favourite worm with Jack.

And Jack shared his biggest
mud pies with Georgie.

Jack shared Georgie's
teddy with the dog.

And Georgie shared Jack's pencils
with the children next door.

At dinner Jack shared
his peas with Georgie.

And Georgie shared
her dinner with the cat.

Georgie shared her
bath with Jack.

And Jack shared his scariest
bedtime story with Georgie.

They both tried to
share Georgie's bed.

Then Jack began to scratch
and itch and scritch and scratch.

“Chicken-pox,” said Mum,
and put him to bed.

And then Georgie began to scratch
and itch and scritch and scratch.

"Do you two have to share everything?" asked Mum.
"Yes!" they said together.
"Especially YOU!"